Two Tales and a Pipe Dream

By Francis Eugene Wood

Cover art and illustrations
Martha Pennington Louis

Acknowledgements

The author would like to thank Jon Marken for his editing and design skills; Martha Pennington Louis for her artwork and willingness to immerse herself in this project at a moment's notice; his parents, grandparents, uncles, aunts, and scores of old storytellers for the truths and fibs they have shared; his wife, Chris, for all she does; and the Great Maker of things, who guides both his pen and his spirit.

In memory of my maternal grandfather

Pinkney Lonzo Clabo
(1898–1983)

Who, as a young man, won a contest in the Great Smoky Mountains with a tale about a chicken and a snake and never failed to light the fires of our imaginations with his wit.

"Spatcheespa!"

A Mermaid Tale

Piadra Orgando was not like other boys who lived in the little village and helped their fathers eke out a living from the sea. He wanted to be like them, but his crippled legs and weak arms would not allow it. His mother would not allow it. "The strain of a fisherman's tasks will be the death of you," she had said.

But Piadra did not believe her. For if he did, then his dreams of voyages and great discoveries beyond the horizon would be dashed. If he believed his well-intentioned mother, he would have to be content mending fish nets and repairing lobster pots beneath shady trees at the sea's edge. He would then spend his days waiting for his father and brothers to return with their boats filled with fish, and their voices boisterous with tales of the sea. Piadra could not live a life so dull. He knew it in his heart. There was more for him. And so he dreamed, and he planned, and he waited.

Piadra's fingers mended and tied the tools of his family's trade, while his mind, which was not crippled in the least, worked within the scope of his desire.

Each week he would set aside most of the money his father would pay him. It was only a small amount, but the man, whose name was Gianni, had great compassion for his youngest son. And perhaps a measure of needless guilt. He would come to the boy's bedside at night and tell of his day at sea. And he would listen with great interest to his son's dreams. But the boy did not tell his father everything. He could not tell him about the little boat he had found, half sunken in a black water eddy. Or how he had repaired it and painted it. He could not mention the boat to anyone. For if he did, he knew his dream would end, and his life would continue mundane and without challenge. That was no life at all for a boy who fancied himself an adventurer, an explorer. He would rather be dead than find contentment in the shade by the sea.

So each day, he worked at his chores. And when he finished them, he walked through the main street of the village to a shanty at the end of a dock, where old fishermen gathered. There he listened to their stories of the sea. He heard of days when the boats returned to the docks so heavy with fish that the sea slurped at their gunnels. And of days so still and quiet that a dying man's whisper could reach them far out at sea. Piadra listened when the old men spoke of signs in the sky, the wind, and waves. Storms they had survived, and fishermen who had been lost forever. He heard of the treachery that lurked in the depths of an emerald beauty. Of watery hands that could snatch a man overboard in the blink of an eye. They spoke of sirens, naked and beautiful, who called men to rocky shores with lustful voices. "Beware of the sirens," they warned the boy. "For their vanity is fed by weak men and lost souls."

The old fishermen were fond of the crippled boy who showed his interest in them. Most of the boys in the village mocked and shunned them. But not Gianni's son, Piadra. He was different and respectful. And so they doted on him and fed him their tales. They had compassion for him, for they knew he would never go to sea. Not a boy so crippled and weak.

But they did not know Piadra's heart, or what drove him beyond what seemed to be his lot in life. They did not understand the strength of his will. Stories they told merely for entertainment were inspirations to Piadra. "I will take my own boat out to sea soon," he confided to his old friends one day. "And I will return with fish spilling over the hatch."

The old fishermen laughed and agreed. "You will bring great wealth to your family, Piadra," one said. "Great wealth indeed."

Another spoke up. "Gianni and his wife will carry pride in the leisure you will afford them. And your brothers will envy your success."

A voice, deep and rugged, settled the chuckles and murmurs that filled the room. "Aye, lad." There was the creaking of a wooden rocking chair and then the sound of its back-and-forth motion on the boarded floor as the source of the voice rose and moved into the smokey sunlight that shone through a window. The interior of the shanty became silent, except for the tall man with a weathered face and a patch over one eye. He stirred the bowl of his pipe with the thin blade of his pocket knife, then emptied its contents onto the floor. He looked out the window toward the sea and then back at Piadra. The boy watched as the big man pinched tobacco from a pouch and packed it into his pipe bowl. He brought the pipe's stem to his lips and struck a match. He cupped his gnarled fingers around the flame and drew on the pipe. Smoke seeped from the corners of his mouth. The flame from the match between draws accentuated the crevices in the man's face and the black depth of his eye. The boy watched as the man blew out the match with a breath of smoke and crunched it in his hand. "Set out early, boy," he advised. "And never let the moon find you alone on the sea at night."

Piadra swallowed and looked at the faces of the old fishermen in the room. Their eyes were focused on the window toward the sea.

The one-eyed man approached him and bent down. Piadra felt drawn into the dark abyss of his stare. "For with the moon come the mermaids and their songs to coax you into the depths forever, no more to be seen by mortals." The man pressed a crooked finger against Piadra's chest, then continued in a rank and raspy whisper. "There's a longing in you, lad. And if I can see it in your eyes, so will the creatures from the deep. Beware of the sealskin cap."

Piadra was mesmerized by the tone of the man's voice. He was submerged in the man's stare, until a wink released him from the dark well of his eye. A ragged chuckle followed the wink. Then the man returned to his rocking chair in the corner of the room.

"Don't mind him, Piadra," a kind voice advised. "He lost part of his mind with his eye. Do not let him frighten you."

"I am not afraid," Piadra said as he opened the door to leave. He paused at the door and looked over at the big man in the rocking chair. A shroud of pipe smoke encircled his face, but Piadra heard the rumble of his voice. "Beware the sealskin cap, Piadra."

Piadra stepped out of the shanty and closed the door behind him. He stood there for a minute and looked out to sea. Then he walked down the main street of the village until he came to a narrow alley. Beyond that was a stony trail that led to an eddy where his boat was hidden. He looked up at the cloudless sky. He lifted a watch from his pocket and was happy to have an hour before his father and brothers would return. Piadra stepped up his pace. There was still much to do.

Time passed, and one morning Piadra arose as usual with his father and brothers. His mother kissed him as he followed his siblings out the door. "There is extra fruit in your lunch pail today, Piadra."

"Thank you," the boy replied. He had told his mother he would not be home for lunch that day. He kissed the woman, and walked out the door.

An hour later, he waved goodbye as his father's boat sputtered toward the sunrise. Piadra sat beneath the tree and busied himself with a torn fishing net until the boat was far from shore. Then he laid the net across a beam and stacked the lobster pots he had repaired. He picked up the lunch pail his mother had given him and headed toward the main street of the village.

Dogs barked in the distance as he came to the alley. He looked behind him as he entered it. He saw no one. By the time Piadra arrived at his boat, two hours of precious daylight was gone. He hurriedly pulled at the fishnet webbing, which had been stuffed with branches and dried grasses to camouflage the boat.

He started the small engine and pulled away from the bank, steering carefully through narrow channels and past sunken logs until, finally, he gained open water. Once out to sea, he avoided distant fishing boats and headed toward an area where the old fishermen had told him the fish were plentiful.

It was midday by the time Piadra shut the boat's engine and threw out his fishing nets. When this task was done, the boy started the engine and trolled against the current. The old fishermen were right. Before long, the holding tank in his boat was brimming with fish. This would be the proof, he thought. His days under the shade tree by the water were over. He was a fisherman. And soon, he would have his own tales of the sea to relate to the boys in the village.

Piadra's arms were tired when he pulled in the nets for the last time. His back ached. He cut the boat's engine and let the vessel drift with the current while he straightened his nets and secured the deck for his triumphant arrival home. But when at last he tried to start the motor, it would not respond. He worked as vigorously as he could, but as darkness began to settle over the sea, the boy sat in his seat and noticed for the first time the swells beyond his boat's gunnels. They were on the verge of becoming waves. The wind blew from the northeast. A flock of seagulls passed overhead, bound for shore. The boy tried again to start the motor, but it was useless. He grabbed an oar and tried to turn the bow of the boat into the swells. But the boat was heavy from his day's catch, and his arms were too weak. Finally, he sat down again, trying his best to calm his fears. He prayed that a boat would come his way and help him. But he knew he had deliberately gone in a direction away from the other fishing boats. Piadra was alone on a sea which was getting angrier by the minute. An hour later, he was holding on for his life, as the sea battered his boat. The violent onslaught continued for hours. Time and again the watery hands of the sea tried to snatch the boy and drag him overboard. But Piadra had tied himself to his seat. Never before had he experienced such rage as that from the sea. He prayed and shouted and cried. He thought of his mother and father. He longed to see his brothers. He remembered the warnings of the old fishermen. Oh, to be in the safety of his room, or under the shade of the tree by the sea. Piadra closed his eyes. He felt shame. He was the one who had wished for a life full of adventure. And now, as the result of his endeavor bore down upon him, he paled at its challenge. Anger arose in the breast of the boy, and with it a strength he had never known. It was defiance. He had worked too hard and had come too far for it to end like this. Sunken and drowned. Piadra grasped the oar and stood up. He loaded it onto the stern of the boat and pulled with all his might to turn the bow into the waves which swept over the vessel. "I'll not let you take me down!" he shouted. "Not this night!"

The wind and sea roared back at the boy. Crashes of thunder and streaks of lightning as he had never heard or seen gave testimony to the rage of nature Piadra could not have imagined. And yet, he stood against it, crippled and weak, yet strong in defiance, until a massive wave nearly capsized the boat. It ripped the oar from his hand and sent the boy sprawling onto the deck. His head struck hard upon the swamped decking. The anger of the heavens dared him to rise, while the sea beckoned him to sink. Piadra tried to stand, but he could not. "I am Piadra Orgando," he called out with his hands raised to the sky, "son of Gianni, a great fisherman, and I will not die like this. I will not!" His words echoed in his head as he slumped to the deck. The raging storm became distant in his mind, as he had reached that place where pain and fear are nonexistent–a blissful place beyond endurance, where the mind shuns reality and care is forgotten.

The storm's roar became a rush followed by a ringing sound. Then silence, tempted by the faint voice of a songstress. Piadra opened his eyes slowly and stared for the longest time at a full moon. Water slurped at the back of his neck as he lay where he had fallen. He raised a hand and touched his face. "I'm alive," he whispered.

"I'm alive." His words were echoed.

Piadra raised his head and looked around. He knew he was alone. A sloshing noise came from over the side of the boat, and Piadra rose and looked into the water. The moon shimmered in its reflection. "I'm alive." He heard the voice again and turned. At that moment Piadra focused upon a scene which would have been more acceptable in a dream. But the boy was not dreaming. He shook his head and blinked his eyes. He spread out his hands and counted his fingers. Then he brought his hands to his face and spied past them. It was a minute or more before he finally spoke. "I hit my head, so I must have awakened a lunatic!" Piadra lowered his hands as he talked. "Surely, you are not really here."

"Oh, but I am here, Piadra," replied the figure before him.

"How do you know my name?"

"You called it out over the storm," answered the figure. "You are Piadra Orgando, son of the fisherman named Gianni. And you are determined not to die this night."

"I didn't die?" Piadra was confused.

"Look at the moon."

Piadra looked up at the full moon.

"Now, feel the deck of your boat."

Piadra thumped the flooded deck boards with the heel of his shoe. Water splashed onto his face. He rubbed the sting from his eyes.

"Touch my hand, Piadra."

Piadra leaned forward and reached toward the outstretched hand of a girl who balanced her upper torso on the gunnel. As their fingers touched, the boy looked upon the moonlit face of the girl. Her beauty was beyond belief. Shadows crept from her eyes. When she smiled, her lips were full and perfect. Her jaw line was strong, yet feminine, and her neck, delicate. She blinked her eyes, and long eyelashes swept the air beneath her brow. A water droplet fell from her eyelash and coursed its way down her face and neck. It disappeared into the strand of a shell necklace that draped over her breasts.

Piadra was mesmerized. He stood up slowly and leaned over the side of the boat. "Where are your clothes?" he asked as he knelt back down on one knee.

"I have no clothes," the girl answered without shame.

"You are a mermaid." Piadra did not have to ask. "And what is your name?"

"I am Arigold," she answered. With a swish of her long tail fin, the mermaid emerged and sat on the gunnel rail.

Piadra was startled, but unafraid. "My boat is sinking, Arigold." Piadra spoke as if he had resigned himself to the reality of his situation.

Arigold agreed. "Yes. There are cracks in its hull. We saw them during the sea's rage."

"We?" Piadra questioned as he looked overboard.

Arigold smiled. "Yes. My sisters and I were racing in the current below when the sea became angry. We heard the creaking of your boat and came to the surface to see what it was that would soon litter the sandy depths. When we saw how small your boat is, we decided to help it stay afloat."

Piadra sighed. "So it was you who kept it from capsizing."

The mermaid shrugged her shoulders. "You would have gone over unless we helped you."

"But why didn't you allow the sea to have its way?"

Arigold looked up at the moon, then back at Piadra. "Because I like your name."

Piadra blinked. No girl had ever complimented him in a way that would show her interest. The village females were generally cruel to him. Piadra was the poor crippled boy who, in their eyes, would never rise above his fate. But they did not know his spirit or what it was that drove him, and they were unaware of his patience. "Where are your sisters now?" he asked.

Arigold flapped her tail fin on the water's surface. "They are gathering the bubble plant that will keep you afloat until we can get you ashore."

"You are kind to help me." Piadra was touched by the mermaid's willingness to rescue him. The boy lifted the latch on the boat's hold tank. He grabbed a fish and was about to throw it into the sea.

Arigold stopped him. "Do not throw away your catch, Piadra."

"It will lessen the weight of my boat," he protested.

Arigold laughed. "There are six of us. It will be no trouble."

Piadra closed the hatch and walked over to the mermaid.

"Come with me, Piadra," she beckoned. "We will swim in the moon's glow."

Piadra was embarrassed. He looked down at his feet. "But my legs are crippled."

Arigold reached into a pouch which hung from a pearl belt around her thin waist. She brought out a cap made of skin and offered it to the boy.

Piadra stepped back, remembering the warning of the one-eyed fisherman.

The mermaid urged him to take it. "With this you will swim as a fish."

Piadra shook his head. "But my arms are weak."

Arigold smiled. "The magic of the sealskin cap will give you the strength to swim against the strongest current."

Piadra looked out upon the shining blackness of the sea. His heart beat fast. "I am afraid," he admitted in a broken voice.

Arigold shook her head. "Afraid?" she questioned. "Not the brave young man who went to sea alone to fish and who stood against the storm." The mermaid looked at Piadra knowingly and smiled. "Your courage summoned us from the depths, Piadra. Your fearlessness brought you here."

Piadra thought about the mermaid's words. He looked into her eyes and felt drawn to her by her wisdom.

"Come with me, Piadra." Her soothing voice and demeanor projected trust.

Piadra took the cap. He pulled it snug onto his head, then turned around and removed his clothes. He heard a splash and looked to see Arigold waiting for him just beyond the bow of the boat.

"The change will come when you enter the sea," she called. "I will be with you, Piadra."

Piadra walked up to the bow of his boat and raised his hands up toward the moon. A gentle sea wind caressed his body. He breathed in the air and with it the courage and trust to dive into the dark and shining sea.

The instant Piadra entered the water, he felt the change. His arms were no longer weak, and his legs became a mighty rudder. He had never known such strength and agility. His weightlessness was a new freedom. He blinked his eyes and a thin film of skin came over them. His eyesight and night vision was unimaginable. Streaks of moonlight shone through the sea's surface, and he watched as Arigold moved toward him, her body so graceful. She swam up to him, smiled and took his hand. Together they swam in the moonlight. He followed her to the sea's floor, where they explored canyons and caves, sunken ships and treasures long forgotten by men.

In a flowing garden miles from his boat, he met Arigold's sisters who were busily gathering the bubble plants. They spoke in mysterious tones, which Piadra somehow understood. The sisters were named Dialga, Florencia, Savenia, Maltesa, and Trishana. And although they were beautiful, none was as beautiful as Arigold.

The time passed quickly, and soon they were all back at Piadra's boat, where they lashed the bubble plants in bundles to the vessel.

Arigold and Piadra then pulled the boat through the water with a rope, while the sisters held to its sides, propelling it forward with each swish of their tail fins.

It was just before dawn when Piadra saw the shore of his village. Fishing boats would soon be leaving the docks. His parents would surely be worried. They and his brothers would have been searching for him. But no one would think to look to the sea for him. How could they imagine he would return from the sea? Not the crippled boy. But gone to sea he had, and more. He would never sit in the shade and watch his father and brothers leave again.

While still at a safe distance from shore, Arigold's sisters bade farewell to Piadra. They would wait for Arigold further out to sea, away from nets and barbs that would harm them.

Arigold and Piadra held hands in the water at the stern of the boat as the sun began its rise from the sea.

"I have fallen in love with you, Piadra," said the mermaid. A tear left the corner of her eye. She reached her arms around Piadra's neck and whispered in his ear. "Come back to me."

Piadra looked into her eyes and kissed her lips. "I will come back to you every day," he promised. "And one day when my work is done among men, I will return to you forever."

Arigold cried softly on Piadra's shoulder and then said, "I will rise for you each day and long for our 'forever'."

Piadra removed the sealskin cap from his head and gave it to Arigold. Then he pulled himself into his boat. The weakness of his body returned. He was crippled again, but he was stronger than ever inside. He used the long rudder to guide the boat to shore.

The little fishing village came to life with the word

of Piadra's return from the sea. No one ever questioned his abilities after that day. He was no longer looked upon as the weak and crippled boy but as a man who rose above his afflictions. He built his own boats and fished the sea with his father and his brothers. And many times, he would go out alone, always to return with a boat filled with fish and even treasures from the deep, like pearls for his mother. Piadra was both a mystery and a legend to the people of his village. No man could match him. No woman could have him.

One day, not long after the passing of his father and mother, Piadra Orgando said goodbye to his brothers and set out to sea in the small boat he had found and repaired as a boy. He had christened it "Arigold." No one ever knew where he heard such a name. And no one ever saw him again.

A Rooster Tale

When I was a boy, I had the opportunity to spend weeks of my summer vacations with my grandparents, aunt and uncle, and their children on their farm outside Farmville, Virginia. Those were great days filled with wonder and new discoveries.

It was during those visits I learned what little I know about farming. I helped my cousins with their chores and had a few of my own. One of those chores was to feed the chickens. I loved to do that. There were laying hens and pullets and roosters. Most of them stayed in a coop. But some were allowed to range freely around the barnyard. There were little hens and a couple of roosters that were pretty and colorful. I threw cracked corn on the ground for those chickens they called bantams. I'd watch them feed and, once in a while, I would come close to catching one. My Uncle Armalee laughed at my efforts and egged me on. He was always teasing me, but he was just about the best uncle a boy could have because he'd take time with me. He'd tell me things, too. Some of what he said I've kept to myself. But there was wisdom mixed

in with all his foolishness. To this day, I have wonderful memories of the farm and my family there.
That's where the story of my unusual pet begins.

One bantam rooster stood out from the others. I
mean, he was a spectacular little bird with plumage,
colorful and rich. The sunlight would change some of
his feathers from green to blue. His comb was bright
red, and his beak was as yellow as a buttercup. A
graceful, perky little king if ever there was one. He
was my favorite, and I tried especially hard to catch
him every day, to no avail.

One day I was playing barefooted in the barnyard
and cut my toe on a plow disc. Uncle Armalee sat me
up on a wooden barrel and cleaned and dressed the
wound. I had cried a little but was trying to be brave.
My uncle said that if I could catch that little rooster
before my parents arrived that day, I could have him. I
guess he thought if I put my mind to an almost impos-
sible task, I wouldn't think about the pain in my toe.

I put on my shoes and went and found that rooster
scratching in the dirt beside a little shed. I watched
him long enough to know he was hungry. So I got a
handful of cracked corn and stuffed it in my pocket.
Then I pulled a chicken crate off the back wall of the
shed. It was heavy, but I managed to drag it to the
corner of the shed and set it on its side, just out of
sight of the rooster. I tied a long piece of baling twine
to the door of the crate, pulled it back, and arranged it
so that it opened toward the barnyard. Then I found
a long, thin board and propped it against the opening
to make a ramp. I covered the ramp with dirt. Next,

I reached into my pocket and brought out the cracked corn. I sprinkled it around inside the open crate and then began a trail of grain down the middle of the ramp, all the way to the corner of the shed. Carefully, I peeked around to see if the rooster was still nearby. He was a sharp little fowl, and I didn't want him to see me. I threw out a few grains of corn and waited to see if he would come after them. In a few minutes, he did. That's when I ran over and crouched behind some hay bales, twine in hand. My heart was racing, but I was as still as I could be. I wanted to take that rooster home with me. After what seemed the longest time, I saw his head bob around the corner of the shed as he pecked at a piece of corn. He stood motionless for a minute, and I was almost sure he could hear my heart pounding. But he didn't, and one-by-one, he began picking up the corn I had left for him. I was surprised when he paid no attention to the ramp I had placed in his path. As a matter of fact, he picked up all the corn on the ramp and hesitated only a second or two before he hopped into the crate. At that moment, I pulled on the twine and you never heard such a racket as the ramp fell against the wooden bars of the crate, and that rooster realized he'd been captured. I ran over to the crate and pushed the door closed. Then I looped the twine around it a couple of times to make sure it wouldn't open.

That rooster flapped his wings and ran back and forth in his little prison. He had forgotten all about the cracked corn. Finally, he hunkered down in a corner. I wanted to touch him, but his beady little eyes had a wildness in them, so I was cautious. I reached around behind him and tried to touch his wing feathers, but he pecked at me and made some threatening sounds I'd never heard a rooster make.

"I got you," I said as I dragged the crate out into the sunshine.

When Uncle Armalee saw my prize, he was impressed. "How'd you catch him?" he wanted to know.

"I tricked him with a trail of cracked corn," I told him.

He let out a raspy laugh and said, "You got you a rooster now, boy!"

I was so proud I could have strutted myself, but I didn't. I was worried that my parents would not let me take him home. Although there was a bit of reluctance at first, my uncle and grandfather convinced them that a boy with such cunning and fortitude surely deserved a bantam rooster of his own.

I always hated to leave the farm when my visits were over, but the day my dad set the crate with my rooster in the back of our 1957 Chevrolet station wagon was an exception. This time I was taking something of the farm back with me.

On the way home, we stopped in Farmville to visit with my other set of grandparents. My dad's brother, Jimmy, and his wife, Audrey, were there when we arrived. Everyone came out to the car to see my rooster. I told the story of how I captured him. They were all impressed, especially my uncle, who tried to coax the rooster to crow with his own hilarious "cocka-doodle-do." The little feathered king nestled in the corner of the crate and looked suspiciously at my uncle. A worried sound came from his beak. I laughed. "He thinks you are the silliest-looking rooster he's ever seen," I said.

"He's just jealous," replied my uncle.

Later on the drive home, I was trying out names on my new pet and had gone through perhaps a dozen when, finally, I said "Jimmy." The rooster, which had not really responded to any of the previous names, immediately cocked his head to the side and looked at me with a beady little eye. "Jimmy," I said again. He made a strange sound, stood up, and began pacing back and forth. "That's it," I said happily. "You weren't impressed with my uncle Jimmy's crowing, but you like his name."

I was always told that a rooster has a very small brain and not a lot of sense. But Jimmy was different. He was bright and attentive, and he opened up to me as soon as he understood that I was his main source for food. I kept him in the crate on a table right outside my bedroom window for about a week. It was a screened-in porch area, so I didn't have to worry about snakes getting to him, or varmints pulling him through the crate bars. His early-morning crowing was an annoyance to my mother. The problem of leaving him on the porch was compounded when Mom's bridge buddies had to pass by what she referred to as "that smelly chicken crate" to get into the house.

So I hauled the crate up onto a canvas awning that covered the breezeway that led to our backyard.

This was a difficult task for a young boy and somewhat tricky, too, as my mother was not fond at all of my habit of climbing onto the roof of our house. She never seemed to understand the vantage point of such a high area when one is continuously on the lookout for Indian war parties or Santa Anna's charging troops.

The long branches of an ancient maple tree swept out over the breezeway and offered shade to Jimmy's crate during the daytime. But it didn't really matter, because within a few days of his relocation, I was leaving the crate door open for him to go and come as he pleased.

Food was not a problem as we lived in the gatehouse of the McRea Farm in Brunswick County, a few miles outside of Lawrenceville. There was a large chicken coop in the barnyard and a feed room where they kept bags of grain and a bin full of chopped corn. I would cross the road and sneak into the feed house once or twice a week and fill a lunch bag with chopped corn for Jimmy. There were horses and ponies on the farm, too, and once in a while I would stop by the tack room and lift a couple of sugar cubes out of a bag in a cabinet. Jimmy didn't eat the sugar cubes, and I didn't have a horse or a pony. But I did like those sugar cubes. I'd drop one in a jar of cold water and lay on the roof of our house and sip sweet water under a shady limb. But don't think I was stealing, because I was born and raised a Southern Baptist, and I can come close to justifying most everything I've ever done. I left a nickel each week on the edge of that grain bin, and it was always gone when I returned. I don't remember paying for the sugar cubes, but then I didn't take that many, and sugar was cheap back then.

Jimmy loved to peck around in the backyard of our house. He'd chase butterflies out of my mother's flower bed, and he seemed to have a passion for scratching in my little brother's sandbox. Mom didn't like it, so I stayed busy chasing him away from it. She said he left things in there, but I never saw Jimmy carry anything around with him, so I wasn't sure what she was talking about.

A high lattice fence encircled our backyard, and much of it was covered with honeysuckle and wild roses. Jimmy loved to roost on top of the lattice. I made a big nest in the honeysuckle, and we'd sit up there sometimes for hours. It was a good vantage point. We spotted many deer behind the house. Groundhogs that came too close to my dad's garden were fair game, and I would pummel them with stones I kept in an empty paint bucket next to our perch. Jimmy was always very alert but stayed close by me. He learned early on that I carried saltine crackers in my shirt pocket for him. I would break off little pieces and feed them to him. If I held him in my arms, he would always try to poke his head into my shirt pocket. You can imagine his confusion and disappointment when I wore only a T-shirt.

The honeysuckle nest was a safe haven for Jimmy whenever Dad's rabbit beagles were let out of their pen. Those little hunters had no tolerance for a shiny, feathered rooster. A couple of close calls taught Jimmy that whenever he saw them coming it was time to take flight. I told him that foxes and bobcats prowled the field beside the house. And that snakes slithered around down below the garden, and hawks with large beaks and sharp talons were always on the lookout for a field mouse or a rabbit or even a little rooster. I saw a hawk swoop in and snatch a squirrel off the side of an oak tree once. One minute that squirrel was busily eating his lunch, and the next minute, he was lunch. I didn't want that to happen to Jimmy. He was more than just a rooster to me. He had become my friend.

Out in the country where I lived, there were not a lot of children to play with. But there was a boy named Ronnie Brewer who lived just up the road from us. Sometimes we'd get together. He had a pet raccoon. But one day while my mother was napping with my little brother, Ronnie and I sneaked into our pantry, climbed up on top of the refrigerator, and ate a whole jar of sweet pickles. One of us spilled the sticky pickle juice down the front and sides of the refrigerator. Then we tracked it through the kitchen as we escaped to run free and wild through the fields and forest. That was the last time I remember playing with Ronnie. Of course, I paid a price for our adventure later, but it was worth it.

Margaret lived in the big house across the road. Besides Jimmy, she was my best friend. We'd talk to each other for hours, she sitting on the fence on her side of the road, and I on my side. Sometimes we'd toss a ball back and forth. When I would venture over to her side of the road, we would climb the magnolia trees in her grandparent's yard. Once we pretended like we were horses and ate all the daisies beside a walkway at the back of her grandparent's house. Her grandmother would usually send me away whenever I'd ask if Margaret could come out to play. I heard her once tell a maid that I was a wild boy. But the maid liked me and gave me cookies and Kool-Aid whenever her employer was out of sight. She'd also let Margaret come out and talk with me.

Mostly, with an older sister and a baby brother, I was on my own. That's why Jimmy was such a good friend.

One of my favorite things to do was to throw Jimmy up into the air as high as I could. He would flap his wings and then glide up into the honeysuckle atop the lattice fence, or onto the roof of the house. I would join him and give him a cracker. Now the house roof was a forbidden area for me, according to my mother. But I did spend a lot of time up there. I could join Jimmy while Mom was busy ironing or caring for my brother. Jimmy would perch on my shoulder and we'd wait for a car or truck to come by. That could be a pretty long wait sometimes. It was so quiet out where I lived that you could hear a vehicle coming long before you saw it. I could hear it crossing the iron bridge over the Meherrin River a half mile away. And when one would come by, I'd stand up and yell like Tarzan of the Apes. If their window was down, usually they would slow down and look up at me. What they would see was a boy with a rooster perched on his head. It must have been a peculiar sight.

One day I counted four cars, two pickup trucks, a pulpwood truck, and a mule-drawn wagon as they passed by the house. I told Jimmy we could make some money with a lemonade stand and photo opportunities if he was up for it.

I set up my mother's bridge table next to the road with a pitcher of ice cold lemonade, brightly colored aluminum cups, and a sign which read, "Lemonade – 5¢ a cup. Photo with rooster – 15¢." I had decided that if five passing vehicles stopped for lemonade, 25 cents was not going to buy much in town. But if they wanted a photo of themselves with the smartest rooster in Brunswick County, then a dollar a day would add up fast in a week's time. I borrowed the family camera, a Brownie Hawkeye. It was a Kodak box camera, black and white film, of course.

I tied a length of baling twine to one of Jimmy's legs and secured it to my wrist. Mom said he couldn't stand on her table, so I just kept him on my shoulder or on the grass instead. With the twine around his leg, I didn't worry about a passing car or truck scaring him into flight.

It was two hours before a truck came by. And that was Margaret's dad, Bill. He bought a cup of lemonade and said he'd give me a dollar for the rooster. I told him Jimmy was not for sale, but I'd take a photo of him with my rooster. He said, "What in the world would I do with a picture of me and Jimmy?"

And I said, "You can tell all of your friends that you're chummy with the smartest rooster in Brunswick County. And here's the proof."

He laughed and said he had hay to cut in the sandy low ground.

Only two other cars came by that afternoon and neither one of them stopped.

Jimmy and I were about to call it a day when I heard a familiar sound coming from around the bend in the road a quarter of a mile away. Robert, the plowman, was in that mule-drawn wagon of his. I told Jimmy we might as well wait and see if Robert was thirsty.

It took forever for him to get to us, but when he did he hollered, "Whoa, here!" to his mule. That mule was sweating and swishing his tail at the horseflies that had followed him down the hill. He looked over at Jimmy, and Jimmy didn't like him a bit. He sat nervously on my shoulder and made some worried sounds.

"Howdy, Mista Francis," Robert said as he came off the wagon. He was always cordial whenever he passed by the house. He was dressed in what I saw as an old dark and ragged Sunday suit. The stained collar of his white shirt was buttoned at the top, and his fedora was pushed back on his head. He looked hot. His eyes were bloodshot with sweat.

"Hi, Robert," I replied. "You been plowing nearby?"

"Sho' have, son," he answered. "I done three gardens already t'day, and I gots two mo' fo' evenin'." Robert looked at the pitcher of lemonade sitting on the table in its own puddle of condensation. "How much fo' a cup, son?"

"Five cents," I said.

Robert pulled on a shoestring fastened to his belt loop and retrieved a leather change pouch from his pocket. He reached in and picked out a shiny quarter.

"I best take two cups," he said as he placed the quarter on the table.

I looked at Jimmy, then back at my house. There was only a nickel in my change tray. "I only have a nickel I can give you for change, Robert," I confessed. "But for a quarter you get two cups and a photo with Jimmy, here."

Robert rubbed the sweat from his eyes with his handkerchief and eyeballed Jimmy. "Dat's one fine rooster, son."

"He's the smartest rooster in Brunswick County," I said proudly.

"Will he peck?"

"No, sir."

Robert smiled. "Well then, I'll have dat photo."

I untied the twine from my wrist and placed Jimmy in Robert's hands. He knew how to hold a rooster. And Jimmy seemed fine with it.

Robert walked over and stood next to his mule. "I'll jest stand here next to Abel," he said.

I found their pose in the window of that brownie camera and snapped the picture. "Come by next week, and I'll have your photo for you," I said.

Robert handed Jimmy back to me. "Now, how do you figure this here is the smartest rooster in the county?" he asked.

I poured him his first cup of lemonade and said, "Well, it was his idea to charge you 15 cents for the photo."

Robert got a hoot out of my answer. He drank his second cup of lemonade and left.

1961

That photo turned out good. And two weeks later, Robert stopped in front of the house, and I ran it out to him. He seemed delighted. I wish I had kept a copy. But when you are a child, you don't think about the things you'll someday miss. That photo with Robert and Abel was the only one ever taken of Jimmy.

Jimmy and I gave up the lemonade stand after that one day. Our country road just didn't have the traffic to sustain our efforts. The summer passed in its normal cycle, but much too fast for a boy. By early September I was back in school, and my long days of freedom and adventure became treasured memories. I tried my best to find interest in my school subjects, but I was born with a wildness that has never been tamed. I did then as I do now. I suffer the expected and relish the unknown. In school I daydreamed of my days afield, cherishing my experiences and imagining my discoveries. A butterfly could flicker by an open schoolhouse window and I would wonder if Jimmy was chasing the darting little teases in the backyard. I worried that he would someday go beyond the yard without me there to protect him. I thought of closing his cage door during the day, but I could not rob him of his freedom, as I had been robbed of mine.

So the days passed, and each time I arrived home and found Jimmy perched on the crest of the rooftop, I was happy and relieved. Jimmy always seemed to be waiting for me to come home. Our friendship did not wane in those days of my absence. And I looked forward to seeing him as one did an old and dear acquaintance. "Never go past the lattice without me," I reminded him each day. "I will always protect you."

To my mother's horror, I have always been drawn to rivers and streams. But her own fear of water is not inherent to me. And even before I learned to swim, I often found myself standing knee-deep in the Meherrin River, very close to currents which could have swept me away.

One warm fall day, Jimmy and I slipped away from the house and headed over the fields and through the woods to the river. I had admired the stories of Huck Finn and Tom Sawyer for some time and decided I wanted to feel the river under my feet. With Jimmy on my shoulder, I dragged several fallen logs of suitable

length to the water's edge and lashed them together
with baling twine as best I could. I had little knowl-
edge of what the best wood for buoyancy was, and
absolutely no experience in raft building or boatman-
ship. I only had an inborn need for new experiences
and discoveries, teamed with a fantastic imagination.

I told Jimmy we would float down past the iron

bridge and then bring the raft to the bank and walk home.

It took all of my strength to pull and push the narrow raft into the water. I was pleased and filled with confidence when it did not immediately sink. The old, dried-out logs seemed to bob up and down like a cork on the water. I stepped onto our raft and pushed away from the rocky bank with a long smooth pole I had lifted from a beaver dam. All seemed well for a minute or so, until the river's current caught the raft and propelled it into a spin I could not correct. I almost lost my balance, panicked, and dropped the pole into the current. I crouched down low as I saw the raft was speeding toward a wall of jagged rocks which pierced the surface enough to split the river's flow. The water turned white there, and the sound was threatening. I held on tight as the raft rammed the rocks sideways. The jolt almost threw Jimmy and me into the cold water, but my firm grasp around the twine binding would not allow it. Our apparent danger was driven home when I saw the water was deep on both sides of the rocks. I looked toward the banks of the river. I even called for help. But there was no one to hear me. I held to the binding and lodged my foot against a sharp rock to keep the raft from going over. I looked down river through sweeping tree branches and saw the iron bridge. If someone could only see me, I thought. But what passerby would stop and look up the river for a foolish boy? Then I remembered the game Jimmy and I had played since the day I brought him home. I untied the twine from his leg with one hand and said, "Fly to the bridge, Jimmy. Don't stop in the trees. Fly!" I shouted as I threw him up into the air. I watched with hope as he glided down the river, just under the canopy of tree limbs and toward the bridge. But my heart fell when he veered off to the right toward the riverbank. I could not see where or even if he landed safely. A car crossed over the bridge, and I yelled as loud as I could. It did not stop.

Minutes passed. My fingers were white and numb from gripping the twine. I was holding my own against the current, but my foot was beginning to slip on the rock. I was afraid of the deep water and the current. I looked hopefully again toward the bridge, but instead of seeing a car or truck, I saw a man leaning against the rail of the iron structure. He was waving his hand frantically and shouting at me. He cradled something under his arm, but I could not tell what it was.

Minutes later, Robert, the plowman, waded out into the river, against the current, and rescued me from my raft. He carried me to the riverbank in his strong arms and set me down gently on a seat of ferns. "How did you find me, Robert?" I asked.

The old man caught his breath as he stood there dripping wet at the river's edge. "I was comin' 'long when Abel snorted and pricked his ears. Den, I seen dat rooster o' yo's struttin' out d' woods." Robert shook his head and smiled. "I figu'd you had t' be close by."

"Where is Jimmy?" I stood up. My legs were still shaking.

Robert pointed toward the road. "He's up dar, at d' wagon wit Abel. I tied him to d' seat."

I thanked Robert for helping me that day. Jimmy and I got to ride back to the apple tree in my front yard on the seat beside Robert. And this time, Jimmy didn't seem to be worried with Abel at all.

We all kept what happened that day between us. I appreciated that. It was a lesson learned.

On a chilly November day soon after my seventh birthday, I was playing in my backyard when I heard Dad's beagles barking. Jimmy was scratching around in Mom's flower bed when the little gang of hunters filed through the open gate into the yard. I barely had time to grab Jimmy up in my arms before they were jumping against my legs. "Fly up to your nest, Jimmy," I said as I threw my friend into the air. He flapped his wings and glided up toward his nest in the honeysuckle. "I'll be up in a minute," I called. I watched him. But instead of landing on top of the lattice as he had done hundreds of times before, he glided over it, his wings batting back and forth in the air. "Jimmy!" I called. I broke away from the beagles and ran through the gateway to the other side of the fence. "Jimmy!" I looked in the garden and ran out into the field. I searched for the rest of the day and for many days afterwards. But all I ever found of my friend was one beautiful tail feather. I keep it in a box of treasures I saved from my childhood days. And every once in a while, I take the feather out, hold it up to the sun, and watch it turn from green to blue.

A Pipe Dream

On a cool summer morning in a year now forgotten a golden streak of sunlight found its way through an open window and across the surface of a small wooden table, where a young woman sat counting coins. Methodically she separated the dimes, nickels, and quarters. There were two silver dollars and a pile of wheat pennies. She laid the silver dollars beside a clay vase which held an arrangement of wild flowers that her husband had given to her that morning before breakfast. She touched the petal of a brown-eyed Susan and studied the pattern of the Queen Anne's lace with her dark eyes. Her delicate lips stretched into a smile as she recalled her morning surprise. Flowers and a poem from a man she loved more than she could ever express. Her husband and soon-to-be-father of her first child.

The deep buzzing sound of a ruby-throated hummingbird outside the window coaxed her from her reverie. She watched the tiny creature as it held still in the air above the pale lavender flowers that drooped from the tall stems of hostas she had planted along the sidewalk in front of her house. "If only I had a nickel for every wing-beat that keeps you still in the air, I could buy him the grandest gift," she said.

The hummingbird darted into the upper branches of a white oak tree which stood like an ancient sentinel near the picket entrance gate. "Go away, then, and leave me to my accounting," she scolded teasingly, as she stacked the pennies in separate columns, ten high.

She felt a movement beneath her rib cage, a flutter of activity that caused her to stop and take a breath. She laid her hand gently over a rolling crease in her dress and smiled. "Easy, darling," she said. "We'll take a walk into the village soon and find just the right gift for your father." The woman began humming a lullaby as she counted the coins.

She thought about the dream she had experienced during the night. In it she had opened the door to her husband's study and found him sitting behind a most luxurious desk with brass desk accessories and a fine typewriter. There were photos of her and children in frames on the wall behind him and rows of certificates and other photos of important people interspersed between shelves of books and trophies. As she approached him, he looked up from an editorial he was writing, leaned back in his chair, and removed a pipe from his lips. He smiled but did not speak as he held the pipe out to her. She took the pipe, holding the warm bowl in her palm and marveling at its beauty. The aroma of its contents was sweet and pleasant.

"It's a fine gift, Sophie," the man said. "But where did you ever find such a pipe?"

She awoke before answering her husband's question. But Sophie Clark could not put the image of the pipe out of her mind. It would be the perfect anniversary gift for him, she thought as she read again the poem he had left her.

"Twenty-three dollars and fourteen cents." Sophie was disappointed. After three years of penny-pinching, she had not even been able to save twenty-five dollars. It took practically every cent her husband made as a reporter for the local newspaper to live. And he would not consider that she should work outside of their home. Such was the pride of Edwin Clark and the reflection of his generation.

But Sophie was determined that on their third anniversary, she would buy him a grand gift. The pipe of her dream would be perfect. But a pipe within her budget would have to do. She had seen them in display windows and under glass counters in Chappell's and Wade's stores in the village. But she could not recall their price range. Only that the cheaper pipes were displayed loosely in wooden mugs or strapped to cardboard backings and hung on the wall. A corncob pipe was the cheapest of all. That was what Edwin puffed on at home when he was pouring over a story. His only other pipe had belonged to his grandfather. It was old and worn, and Edwin would only light it up occasionally when he relaxed in the shade of the oak tree.

But Sophie just knew that someday her husband would be the editor of his own newspaper, and he would have to look successful, from the clothes he wore to the house he lived in. And the pipe he smoked would reflect his taste. These were the things that were in Sophie's mind, for she was young and just beginning the journey of life.

Sophie was putting her money in her purse when she heard the distant ringing of a bell and the sound of a rickety wagon coming around the bend in the road. She looked out the window and watched as a black horse came into view. Drawn behind the horse was a colorful wagon with a driver who seemed old and bent forward, his elbows resting on his knees. The wagon was painted light blue, and written in an arc above a brightly-colored rainbow were the words "Mr. Blue Sky's Goods and Remedies."

The horse came to a halt in the shade of the oak tree, and the driver set the brake of the wagon and came off his seat like a man much younger than his years.

Sophie stood up and walked to the front door. When she opened it, the old man was standing at her front steps, smiling at her, his hat in his hands.

"Hello, young lady, I am Mr. Blue Sky," the man said with a wink.

Sophie was taken with the old man's cheerful engagement. She raised her voice to speak, as the songbirds seemed louder than normal.

"Mr. Blue Sky?" she asked.

The man looked back at the oak tree and gave a slight wave of his hand. The songbirds quieted. "Yes, madam, Blue Sky." He pointed up. "Just like the sky up there."

Sophie smiled and raised a brow.

He snapped his fingers in the air. "It's easy to remember."

Sophie laughed and held out her hand. The old man's grasp was cool and gentle. Sophie felt comfortable in his presence. She looked past him at his wagon. "Remedies," she said. "You are a peddler, then?"

"You could call me that," he responded. "But I sell much more than remedies."

The young woman's curiosity was piqued. "Oh? Such as?" She stepped off the porch.

The peddler moved to the side and let her pass. "Allow me to show you," he said as he fell in behind the woman.

"What a handsome animal." Sophie paused at the black horse and rubbed his jaw. She spotted her reflection in his eye. "What's his name?"

Mr. Blue Sky unlatched the side of his wagon, pushed it up and, propped a sturdy blue pole under each corner. He pulled a drawer-like handle and a narrow counter appeared. The wagon's contents were exposed.

"Matthew is his name," he answered. "But I call him Matt for short."

Sophie rubbed the underside of the horse's jaw. "He seems gentle. How old is he?"

The peddler patted the horse on its rear. "Oh, I guess Matt's about five years old. I've been doing this a long time and have had a number of horses over the years. Matt's a good one. He the sixth, you know.

"My goodness!" Sophie did the numbers in her head. Even if the old peddler kept horses for ten years each, it meant he had probably been on the road for at least fifty years.

"How long have you been a peddl..., I mean a traveling salesman?" She asked her question as she walked over to the open wagon.

"For more years than I can count, young lady." Mr. Blue Sky pulled open a long tray of jewelry as he spoke.

Sophie's eyes were wide with wonder. She looked at rings and bracelets and pearl earrings. Never had she seen so many beautiful objects in one place. Inside were racks of clothing and shelves with blankets and bedding. Kitchen utensils and pots and pans hung on hooks from the ceiling. There were jars of hard candy and licorice, Bibles and books of poetry. Beautifully framed paintings sat in a wooden bin next to a shelf containing jars of honey and jugs of molasses.

The old peddler pulled out tray after tray until Sophie finally said, "Wait!" She examined the display with keen interest. "There it is!" Near the center of an array of dozens of pipes, she saw the one in her dream. She stood there in the shade of the oak tree, next to the old peddler she had never seen before, and touched the very object she thought she would never find. "Tell me about this pipe, Mr. Blue Sky," she said as she held it in her hands.

The old peddler looked with a knowing eye at the mesmerized young woman standing next to him. He saw how carefully she handled the pipe and how she could not lift her eyes from it.

"Ah, it is a dandy, Sophie," he began. In all my years, never have I seen one like it. See the beautiful grain? The pipe is carved of briar root from the Mediterranean coast. Hard and aged, it will last a lifetime. The rim of the bowl is fitted with a ring of meerschaum, glued and secured with brass pegs. Its stem is fitted with a quarter-bent bit for the comfort of a man who takes his pipe at leisure. The maker of this pipe was a consummate artist who must have known a certain individual would someday own it." When the peddler finished his explanation, he closed the other drawers and looked at the young woman. "Would you like to purchase this pipe for your husband?"

"How much is it, sir?" Sophie's eyes did not leave the pipe as she spoke.

"I will sell you this pipe for twenty-four dollars," he answered without hesitation. "And I will throw in its lined wooden case and a small bag of pipe tobacco free of charge."

Upon hearing the price of the pipe, Sophie's heart sank until she thought that there might be a few pennies and perhaps a dime or a nickel hidden in the house somewhere.

"Will you be staying in the village for a while, Mr. Blue Sky?"

The old man recognized a controlled desperation in her tone.

"I will be at the end of your road, next to the highway, until the end of the day," he answered. "But if you'd like, I'll come back by before dark."

"Oh no, please. I will come to your place at the intersection today and purchase the pipe." Sophie reluctantly placed the pipe back in its case and nervously rubbed the palms of her hands over the front of her dress.

"But I see no car, madam, and you are, well...."

Sophie blushed and smiled as the man finished speaking.

"Are you sure you can get to the intersection and back?"

"Oh, yes," Sophie was quick to answer. "I walk there and back each day for exercise. And besides, I want it to be a surprise for my husband. It's our third anniversary."

"I understand, then." Mr. Blue Sky closed the drawer and removed the poles that held up the side wall of the wagon. He latched the side securely, then turned to Sophie. "I will see you later today at the end of your road. Be watchful along the way."

"I will be there, sir," Sophie answered in a determined voice.

The peddler pulled himself up onto his wagon seat and released the wheel brake. "Good day to you, Sophie Clark." He tipped his hat. "Let's go now, Matt," he said with a light jerk on the reins.

Sophie watched the peddler pull away. She could hear the rickety wagon wheels and the bell ringing even as he disappeared around the curve in the road. She stood there, alone in the shade of the oak, for the longest time, thinking about the wonderful pipe and the old man with the strange name. She could not fathom how he had known her name, for she was sure she had not told him. But it was a matter of small concern, for there was a search to be conducted throughout the Clark household.

Sophie searched under books and papers in drawers. She looked for coins which might have been dropped and wedged between the floorboards of her entrance hall. She actually found two pennies in this manner. She also found two nickels which had fallen behind the cushions of a settee in the parlor.

By mid-morning, Sophie was tired, so she sat at the window of her bedroom and looked at the nickels and pennies she had found. "Twelve cents," she said under her breath. "I can't even...." She stopped in mid-sentence and stared across the room. A memory came to her, and she rose and walked over to her bedside table, stooped down, and retrieved a Bible from a shelf below the drawer. Its cover was worn and dusty. She blew at the dust and wiped the cover clean with her sleeve. Then she walked back to the window and sat down. She opened the Bible and read her mother's name, which was beautifully written, although the ink had faded. Sophie touched the letters with her fingers and felt a tinge of sadness and longing. She closed her eyes and tried to picture her mother's face. But the image would not appear. She walked over to her jewelry box and searched desperately for a small locket. For a moment, she feared she had somehow lost it. But finally she found it in the tangle of imitation jewelry. She breathed a sigh of relief and walked back to her chair beside the window. She held the locket in the sunlight and rubbed it with her thumb. Then she opened it and saw the faces of her mother and father. Peacefulness came over her as she recalled their voices. She could again imagine the gentle smile of her mother and the quiet strength of her father. She laid the open locket on the table beside the family Bible and began turning the pages of the book she seldom took time to look at. Here and there she would pause and read a scripture. And then she found the book of Matthew. The Sermon on the Mount. It had been her mother's favorite book of the Bible. Sophie recalled as a child asking her mother why. The woman's answer was, "Because the key to heaven and a life fulfilled is found there."

Sophie turned to Matthew 5 and began reading. When she turned the page to the sixth chapter, her mouth flew open in amazement. Within the fold of the page was a ten-dollar bill. She removed the gift and placed it in her apron pocket. Then she did something she had not done in years. She read her mother's favorite chapter of the Bible.

When Sophie left the house, she felt good inside. Her financial woe had been resolved. She could now afford the beautiful pipe for her husband.

But there was something else. Something she would have found difficult to explain. That something had come from words she had read in her room that day, words she knew in her heart were true. Lessons that, if learned and applied, would change a person.

There was a lightness in Sophie's stride as she walked along the dirt road. Her senses seemed heightened. The fragrance of wild flowers brought a smile to her face. And the drone of nature awakened her childhood curiosity. She touched the swell below her waistline and felt an anticipation for a day when she would see the face and hear the voice of the child she carried.

Sophie looked at her watch. There was still plenty of time to buy the pipe and get back home long before Edwin got off work. She so wished to surprise him with the beautiful gift.

She was halfway to the intersection when the sky darkened and the wind began to blow. So suddenly did the storm come upon her that she did not know whether to continue or turn back. Large raindrops had begun pelting her head and shoulders when she heard a voice call to her from the pine wood just beyond the edge of the road. It was a woman's voice. "Come and take shelter with us." Sophie could make out the form of the woman through the sheets of rain. Behind the woman she saw a shelter of pine boughs. After only a slight hesitation, Sophie left the road and entered the woods. Within a few seconds, she was standing beneath the leafy shelter with a young woman and two children, a girl and a boy. The woman was dressed in a worn and faded-flowered dress. Her dark hair was wet and disheveled. A long strand of it was matted to her forehead. The woman was busy adjusting a pine bough when Sophie came under it. "Thank you for the shelter," Sophie said as she touched her wet face with her arm sleeves. "I didn't see this one coming."

The woman smiled. She finished her task and replied. "We are on our way to Norfolk to see my sister. She has found work for me there."

"But where is your car?" Sophie was surprised to find a woman and two children on the side of the road under a make-shift shelter and no car or man nearby. "Are you on your own?" she asked.

The woman smiled through a worried face. She knelt down and pulled a damp blanket up around the shoulders of her children. "There now," she said to the shivering youngsters. "We'll be all right. Mom's gonna take care of you."

Sophie felt compassion for the family and sat down on the ground beside the little girl. "We'll sit close together and keep warm," she said.

The woman sat down beside her son and rearranged the blanket so that Sophie was not left out.

"I had a job in Roanoke," the woman began. "But it wasn't enough to pay the rent, and I couldn't find anything but shameful work."

The little boy sneezed.

"Bless you," Sophie said while reaching for a handkerchief in her bag. "Here," she offered it to the boy.

The woman continued. "Their daddy died last year with cancer, and we've just been hanging on and doing the best we can."

"I'm so sorry." Sophie noticed the girl leaning against her. "My name is Sophie Clark," she announced. "What are your names?"

"Tell Sophie your names, children," the woman urged.

"My name is Jenny," replied the girl.

"And my name is Tim." The boy smiled as he followed his sister's introduction.

The woman extended her hand. "My name is Paula. It's nice to meet you, Sophie."

Sophie shook Paula's hand. "You are a pretty good distance from Norfolk, you know."

Paula agreed. "Yes, we had hoped to be there by evening. But we got as far as the intersection." She pointed down the road. "I figured we'd hole up here for the night and then try and catch a ride east tomorrow. We used to camp some when my husband was alive. And I could've made a fire if it hadn't rained."

Sophie looked at the woman who had offered her shelter. She sensed the fear beneath her veil of pride and strength. Premature grey invaded her otherwise dark hair. A blameless tragedy, wounded yet determined to succeed, Paula was a princess in a pauper's dress, and her children's hope.

Sophie saw the dark circles under the children's eyes. Their worry was obvious. She put her arm around them and prayed silently for the passing of the storm.

Finally the rain ceased, and the forest became quiet, except for the droplets of water that fell like liquid diamonds from the tips of long pine needles. Sunlight found its way again to the forest floor, and tall tree trunks stood enshrouded in a still, light mist. Songbirds began to sing.

The women and children watched and listened until Sophie smiled and said, "There now. Our beautiful day has been sent back to us."

Paula pulled the blanket from the shoulders of her children. She ran her fingers through Tim's curly hair and reached over and touched her daughter's cheek. "See, I told you the storm would pass soon," she said in a soft voice. "Don't worry."

Sophie stood up and straightened her dress. "My house is up the road a short distance on the right side. It's a two-story, with a white picket fence and a large oak tree in front. I want you to go there and wait for me."

Paula rose to her feet and looked at Sophie. "I don't want to impose on you, Sophie," she said apologetically. "I mean, you hardly know us, and…."

Sophie reached out and touched the woman's arm. "I know that you and your children need food and a place to stay tonight. And my home is open to you." She smiled and winked at the children. "And it's not even a ten-minute walk from here."

Paula looked down at the faces of her children, then back at Sophie. Her soft voice was thick with emotion as she spoke. "We'll go and wait at your home, Sophie. Thank you."

Sophie stepped out from under the shelter. She looked up and let the sun touch her face for a moment. A good feeling welled inside of her. "Go and make yourselves comfortable," she said. "I'll be there shortly."

Sophie walked out of the misty pine forest and stepped onto the road that led to the intersection. She walked along with renewed vigor as she thought about her house guests and her good fortune of finding them when she had.

Sophie glanced at her watch and was amazed at what little time had passed since she left her house that morning. Minutes seemed like hours, and total strangers had somehow gained her trust. It was a pleasant confusion in her mind.

A turn in the road brought to Sophie's eyes a page from a child's storybook, as a small rainbow formed from the sun and mist. Its colorful arc hovered over the narrow road. The young woman stood still, in awe. She had never seen a rainbow so close and vivid. She had only imagined the end of rainbows. But here she could see that one end descended onto wet, sparkling treetops, and the other upon the shoulders of an old woman who sat upon a tree stump on the opposite edge of the forest. The shoulders of the old woman were slumped, and she seemed sad.

Sophie approached her slowly. When she came

close enough, she noticed that the woman held a broken cane across her knees. She was shaking her head and mumbling when Sophie spoke to her. "Are you all right, M'am?"

The old woman raised her head and looked at Sophie. "How did you find me, dear?" she asked as if she had expected someone.

Sophie walked closer and answered. "There is a rainbow on your shoulders."

The old woman's eyes widened, and she turned her head from one side to the other. Then she looked up over her head and laughed. "So it is," she said. "A rainbow is on my shoulders. That's funny."

"It's amazing," replied Sophie.

The old woman reached up with one hand and playfully grabbed at the misty colors. "Yes, it's amazing and funny that I can hold up a rainbow but cannot seem to hold myself up without my cane." She lowered her shoulders again and looked at the broken stick lying split across her knees.

Sophie looked at the broken cane. It was old and thin, with many turns in it. Its bent handle was dark from years of use.

"It looks like it was a fine walking cane."

The woman nodded her head. "Yes, it was until it broke."

Sophie studied the ancient hands of the woman and saw a hint of beauty beneath the creases in her face. Her neatly-kept hair was grey with silver highlights. And her eyes were amazingly blue and youthful. "Where are you from?" Sophie inquired.

The old woman looked down the road. "I came from the intersection," she answered. "I'm going to visit my son near the coast."

Sophie was puzzled. She could not imagine why an old woman would be alone on a country road. Perhaps the woman was confused. Sophie's heart went out to her. "What is your name?"

The woman smiled. "My name is Mary."

Sophie laid her hand on the woman's shoulder. "I'm Sophie Clark," she said. "And I want you to wait here until I come back. My house is nearby, and I will take you there."

"Oh, you mustn't worry with me, Sophie," protested the woman. "I will be fine as soon as I find a stick to lean on."

Sophie bent down and looked into the woman's eyes. "Mary, I will help you. Let me."

"Thank you, Sophie," she said softly. "I will wait here."

Sophie left the woman where she had found her and continued her walk to the intersection. It is not far now she thought as she quickened her pace. She looked at her watch. Only a couple of minutes had passed since she last checked. She shook her wrist and brought the watch up to her ear. She could hear it ticking.

Mourning doves cooed from their perches on shallow pine branches as Sophie came around another bend in the road. A toad leaped across a muddy runoff. Sophie saw the little creature. Her senses were attuned to her surroundings in a way that made her

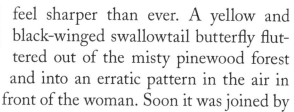 feel sharper than ever. A yellow and black-winged swallowtail butterfly fluttered out of the misty pinewood forest and into an erratic pattern in the air in front of the woman. Soon it was joined by a dark-winged swallowtail, and together they danced in the sunlight for a moment until they ventured off toward the left side of the road.

Sophie watched them as they leaped and fell in graceful abandonment. She saw them enter the forest, where they lit on the ground at the feet of a young man who sat alone and still upon a seat of ferns.

At first Sophie was reluctant to approach the young man, but as she watched him, she somehow knew he needed her help. "Hello," she said as she walked toward him.

The young man lifted his head and immediately Sophie realized he was blind. His face was handsome, and his expression gentle and kind. Sophie was not turned off or afraid of his glazed eyes.

"Hello," the young man responded. His voice was deep. "How did you find me?"

"The butterflies led me to you. My name is Sophie Clark. What's your name?"

"I'm David."

Sophie noticed that the young man was well-dressed. But his shoes were wet and muddy. He seemed calm but tired.

"Where are you from, David?"

The young man seemed confused for a moment. Then he answered. "I'm going home to my parents.

They live on the Eastern Shore. It's been a long time since I've seen them."

"Oh, I see." Sophie was concerned for the young man. "But why are you here on this road?" she asked.

David pulled at his fingers nervously. "I've lost my harmonica," he finally said.

"Your harmonica?" Sophie looked around on the ground.

"Yes. I play the harmonica in a blues band, and I had it with me when…." The young man paused for a moment, then went silent.

"What?" Sophie was intrigued. "Did something happen?"

David raised his face to Sophie and repeated himself. "I've lost my harmonica, Sophie."

It was obvious that David was somewhat confused, and Sophie was sure there was more to his story. She studied his posture and limbs and was confident that he wasn't hurt. She looked up and down the road. She thought about Paula and the children at her house, and about Mary, who was waiting for her to return. Then she thought about Mr. Blue Sky and the beautiful pipe she wanted to buy for Edwin.

She knelt down in front of the blind man and touched his hand with hers. "Listen to me, David. My house is right up the road. I'm going to leave you for just a few minutes and when I return, I will take you there. We'll see about your harmonica and then get you home. Okay?"

David put his hand over Sophie's. She felt a calmness in his touch. "I'll wait for you, Sophie."

Sophie left with the butterflies still at David's feet.

When finally she arrived at the intersection where she found Mr. Blue Sky's wagon, she knew it must be later than her watch showed. For the walk had only taken her the fifteen minutes it usually required. She shook her wrist again and held the watch up to her ear as she approached the wagon.

"Hello there, Sophie." Mr. Blue sky greeted her as he stepped down and out of the wagon's interior. "Glad you made it, young lady."

Matt was unharnessed and grazing freely on grass nearby. He snorted and raised his head as Sophie approached.

"Hello, Mr. Blue Sky. I'm sorry I'm so late getting here."

"Oh, you're not late at all. There are no set times when you are dealing with me." The old man chuckled as he pulled out the tray which held the pipe he knew the woman wanted. He lifted the pipe from its case and handed it to Sophie. She held it as if it was a precious object. She could imagine the look on Edwin's face as he opened his gift. Then other visions came into her mind, and she handed the pipe back to the old peddler.

"Wrap it up for you, Sophie?" he asked.

Sophie looked at the pipe and then at the man. "Not right now, Mr. Blue Sky." She looked up on the walls and along the shelves of the open wagon and saw a banjo and guitar. There was a trumpet and an accordion. There were juice harps and small percussion instruments. "Do you have a harmonica?" she finally asked.

"A harmonica?" Mr. Blue Sky looked at Sophie with a serious expression.

She felt the intensity of his stare, but it did not bother her. "Yes, a harmonica, such as one would play in a band."

Mr. Blue Sky reached up and brought down a black leather case from the back of a shelf. He opened the case and showed the harmonica to Sophie.

"Is it a good one?" she asked.

The peddler nodded. "Oh, Sophie, it's the best buy for the money."

"I'll take it, then." Sophie stepped over to a barrel which contained walking sticks and canes. She picked through the assortment as Mr. Blue Sky stood by. Finally, she chose one that resembled the one Mary had broken. "What wood is this cane made of?"

"It's made of aged hickory. You couldn't break it if you tried. And it's light, too."

"I'll take that, too." Sophie moved over to a rack of clothing.

Mr. Blue Sky peered over his spectacles at the young woman. "Now, we've got you down for one harmonica and the cane. How about that pipe, Sophie?"

Sophie had now laid a flower print dress over her arm and was picking out children's clothing when she answered, "We'll see."

The old peddler waited until the young woman handed the dress and the children's outfits to him. "Add it all up, Mr. Blue Sky," she said.

The old man did his figuring, then looked over his spectacles at Sophie. "Do you want me to figure in the pipe?"

Sophie looked at the beautiful pipe and then at the harmonica, cane, and clothes. "How much is it without the pipe?" she asked.

The man adjusted his spectacles and cleared his throat. "Thirty-one dollars and fifty cents."

Sophie looked at the pipe again and imagined Edwin smoking it at his desk. She smiled and pushed it away. "Not this time. Other things have come up." Sophie looked directly into the eyes of the peddler as she spoke.

He nodded. A smile creased his lips, but he did not speak.

Sophie reached into her purse and handed him the money for her purchases. "Thank you, Mr. Blue Sky," she said as she turned to leave. "I hope you have had a good day today."

"Thank you, Sophie. It has been a fine day, indeed."

The old peddler looked at the pipe. Then he stepped down out of the wagon and stood beside Matt as Sophie walked away. "It's time to pack up, Matt," he said as he rubbed the horse's nose. "We've got a long way to go."

Sophie found David and Mary where she had left them and helped them up the road to her house. They were greeted by Paula and her children under the shade of the oak tree in the front yard. Sophie was astonished that only an hour had passed since she began her walk that morning. It was not yet noon when she presented Paula with a new dress and the children with their outfits.

"I can't tell you what a comfort you have been to us, Sophie," Paula said as the adults sat on the porch steps and Jenny and Tim played around the oak tree. "They were so frightened, and I felt lost."

Sophie put her arm around the shoulder of the woman.

"And I don't know what I would have done if you hadn't found me, Sophie." Mary looked up at a passing cloud, then turned her youthful blue eyes toward Sophie. "I can't walk a step without my cane. And this one is perfect."

David reached out his hand toward Sophie, and she took it. She felt him give her hand a slight squeeze. "I don't know how you found my harmonica. But I'm thankful you did. I've never gone anywhere without it."

Sophie did not know what to say. For there was a feeling inside her that was beyond words. She felt as if it was she who should be thankful. "I wish you all would at least let me prepare a meal for you," she finally said.

No one was hungry.

The hours passed, and in that time there were stories, tears, music, and laughter.

Near mid-afternoon, the children became quiet out by the gate of the picket fence.

"Listen," said David. "Do you hear it?"

"What, David?" Sophie noticed that Paula and

Mary were walking out to the gate. She stood up and looked down the road. She could hear nothing.

"It's the bell, Sophie," David said as he stood up. He put out his hand and gestured for Sophie to guide him. Slowly she walked him toward the others. "What bell?" she asked.

"He's coming," was all that the young man would say.

Sophie wondered whom they were waiting for until finally she heard the bell that hung on the armrest of Mr. Blue Sky's seat. "You all know the peddler?" she asked as Matt pulled the wagon and its driver around the bend.

No one answered. But Sophie could sense a peacefulness among her friends. They waited quietly. The children were holding their mother's hands.

"Whoa now, Matthew," called Mr. Blue Sky as he pulled under the shade of the oak tree. He tipped his hat. "Hello, folks, Sophie."

"You know these people, Mr. Blue Sky?" Sophie was incredulous.

The old peddler smiled and winked at the youngsters. "Of course I know them," he said while making a place beside him on the seat. "Come on up, children."

Without prodding or a look behind, Tim and Jenny climbed up onto the seat next to the man.

"Now Paula, you can step up here and sit on this seat behind the children if you wish. It's small but cushiony."

Paula turned to Sophie and embraced her. "Thank you," she said.

Sophie could not speak. She watched Paula climb onto the wagon.

Mr. Blue Sky climbed down from the wagon and opened a narrow side door. "Mary, I've got a couple of chairs at the back, and I left the back window open so you and David won't be sitting in the dark." The peddler stood at the door to help the woman and man into the wagon.

Mary hugged Sophie and patted her gently on the stomach. "You'll be a wonderful mother, dear. Enjoy every minute with your family."

"I will, Mary," was all Sophie could say.

"I'll play a tune as we leave," David promised with an embrace. "Thanks for helping me."

Sophie bit her lip and tried hard to hold back her tears. She could not believe her friends were leaving. She wasn't ready for them to go. They hadn't even met Edwin.

When the peddler had seated Mary and David in the wagon, he stepped out into the shade of the oak and took a deep breath. "I love big trees," he said as he gazed into the upper branches.

"How do you know these people?" Sophie spoke directly but quietly so the children would not hear.

"I've always known them," responded the peddler. "It's my job."

"But where are you taking them?"

The old man smiled, then reached into his pocket and pulled out the case that held the beautiful pipe. He reached out and placed it in Sophie's hand. "Here's Edwin's gift. Yours waits elsewhere." Mr. Blue Sky's eyes danced with life. He touched Sophie's cheek with his finger and stepped up onto the wagon.

"But I didn't pay for it." Sophie offered to return the pipe.

"Consider it paid in full, young lady." Mr. Blue Sky tipped his hat. "Let's go, Matt," he said. "We've got places to go, and people to see."

The wagon pulled away as David began playing a tune on his harmonica.

Sophie stepped behind the wagon to wave goodbye. She was close enough to see his face as he played with his eyes closed.

"Goodbye, Mary." Sophie said her farewells as she walked behind the wagon. "Goodbye David."

The young man opened his eyes and waved with one hand. That is when Sophie realized his eyes were as blue as the sky. "Goodbye, Sophie," he called.

Sophie walked over and leaned against the picket fence. She listened to the music and the bell until Mr. Blue Sky's wagon was out of sight. Then she opened the case and looked at the beautiful pipe. She became aware of the time and noticed she had just enough to wrap the present and fix supper before Edwin got home. She put away her thoughts and went inside.

Hours later, Sophie walked into the parlor to find her husband sitting in his chair by the open window. She was proud to see that he was admiring the pipe she had given him.

"It's the most unique pipe I've ever seen, honey," he said as his wife sat in a chair, facing him.

"I just knew you would love it." Sophie sensed an

unusual quietness about her husband. She watched him lay the pipe on the window seat and gaze out into the darkness.

"What's wrong, Edwin?" she asked. She knew that his silence was usually a prelude to concern.

"Something happened today, Sophie. Something that made me sad."

"What was it?"

"An accident." Edwin's voice was low.

"What kind of accident?"

"A passenger bus ran off the road and hit a tree down at the intersection."

Sophie raised her hand to her mouth. "Was anyone hurt?"

Edwin swallowed before he answered. "Five people were killed."

Sophie looked out into the darkness. "Do you know their names?"

"Right now all we know is that an elderly woman, a young man, and a mother and her two children were killed."

Sophie did not speak for a while. Her thoughts were too complicated. Her feelings too deep. Finally, she cleared her throat. "When did it happen?"

"Just before 10:00 am."

"Were you there?"

"I was there minutes after it happened and stayed until they towed the bus off and removed the bodies."

Sophie thought back over the events of her morning, then asked the question which was foremost in her mind. "Did you see an old peddler with a wagon at the intersection today?"

Edwin looked surprised. "No. I haven't seen a peddler around here in a long time. Why?"

Sophie shook her head slowly. "No reason."

She rose from her chair and bent over and kissed her husband.

Edwin squeezed her fingers tenderly. "Thank you for my pipe. I'll be upstairs in a few minutes."

Sophie put off the inevitable as she prepared for bed. Finally she opened her purse and looked. It was all there, every cent. Thirty-three dollars and twenty-six cents.

Later that night as she lay in the arms of her husband, she wondered about her day. She thought about Mr. Blue Sky and the souls she had comforted. She wondered, why her? She looked over at the Bible she had left on the bedside table and knew that the answer was there. She felt the life move inside her and closed her eyes. "Why not?" she whispered.

Titles by Francis Eugene Wood

The Wooden Bell (A Christmas Story)
The Legend of Chadega and the Weeping Tree
Wind Dancer's Flute
The Crystal Rose
The Angel Carver
The Fodder Milo Stories
The Nipkins (Trilogy)
Snowflake (A Christmas Story)
The SnowPeople
Return to Winterville
Winterville Forever
Autumn's Reunion (A Story of Thanksgiving)
The Teardrop Fiddle
Two Tales and a Pipe Dream

These books are available through the author's
website: www.tipofthemoon.com
Email address: fewwords@moonstar.com

Write to:
Tip-of-the-Moon Publishing Company
175 Crescent Road
Farmville, Virginia 23901

Francis Eugene Wood is an award-winning Virginia author who lives in Buckingham County. He has been called "imaginative," "prolific," and a "natural storyteller." His books are released through Tip-of-the-Moon Publishing Company, a company he owns and operates with his wife, Chris.